SCOOBY-DOO!
Mystery #1
The Hotel of Horrors

by
Kate Howard

illustrated by
Duendes del Sur

SCHOLASTIC INC.
New York Toronto London Auckland
Sydney Mexico City New Delhi Hong Kong

ISBN 978-0-545-38676-0

12 11 10 9 8 7 6 5 4 3 2 1   12 13 14 15 16/0

Designed by Henry Ng

Printed in the U.S.A.   40

First printing, January 2012

CHAPTER 1

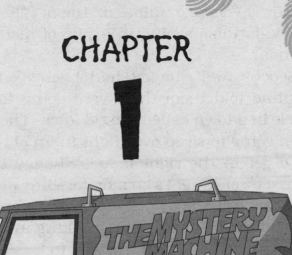

"**A**re we driving to, like, the *middle ages*?" Shaggy moaned. He was wrestling with Scooby-Doo in the back of the Mystery Machine. "You didn't tell us it would take four hundred years to get to Castle Rock."

"Reah," Scooby-Doo whimpered. He peeked out from under a knight's helmet.

"You're the wise guys who decided to wear

armor," Velma reminded them. "It must be uncomfortable sitting in a pile of metal for over an hour."

Scooby and Shaggy had been excited when Daphne told them they were going to visit her uncle in a town called Castle Rock. The gang was even going to sleep overnight in an old castle.

To get in the right mood, Shaggy had found two sets of knight's armor for him and Scooby to wear. But the armor was uncomfortable, and he and Scooby had been clanking and crashing against each other all the way to Castle Rock.

Suddenly, Daphne pointed. "Look! There it is!" The van crested a big hill. There was a beautiful old town nestled in the valley below them. "I

can't wait to see Uncle Brad. It's groovy that he's letting me interview him for the school paper."

"I'm really looking forward to a tour of the police station," Fred said, steering the van carefully down the hill.

"I sure hope we'll get some new tips for solving mysteries," Velma added. "Do you think they have a crime lab at the police station?"

Daphne's uncle was the police chief in Castle Rock. He had agreed to give the gang a tour of the police station. He was also going to talk to them about some of his recent cases.

Shaggy's stomach rumbled noisily through his armor. "Like, I just hope they have a cafeteria."

"Ror ronuts!" Scooby added, licking his lips.

"Donuts! Hey, Fred, let's make this horse go a little faster!" Shaggy cried.

A few minutes later, Fred eased the Mystery Machine into a parking spot between two squad cars. There were television news vans and reporters standing outside the police station.

"I wonder what's going on," said Daphne, frowning.

"Daphne!" A short, burly-looking man shouted over the news reporters. He waved them over. "Come on inside the station."

The gang pressed past the reporters and into

the busy police headquarters. Scooby and Shaggy were still wearing armor. Everyone stared at them as they scraped and clanked through the station.

"Gang, this is my uncle Brad Bestler," Daphne said.

"It's a pleasure to meet you, Chief," Fred said, shaking his hand. "Thanks for inviting us here to Castle Rock."

"Things are a little nutty in town at the moment," Uncle Brad said. "I'm afraid I'm not going to be able to show you around today."

"No problem," Shaggy said. "You can just point us in the direction of the donuts."

"Do you have a big case to solve?" Velma asked. "Anything we can do to help?"

Uncle Brad frowned. "We have a case I just can't seem to crack," he said sadly. "Someone has stolen valuable jewels from the art museum, a gallery, and several homes in Castle Rock. It's the strangest thing . . ." He trailed off, shaking his head.

"What's strange?" Velma pressed.

"Well, I just don't know what to make of it," Uncle Brad said. "All the jewels have been taken from different places on different nights. But we don't have any real clues. The thing is—" He lowered his voice to a whisper. Fred, Daphne,

Velma, Shaggy, and Scooby all leaned in close to hear him. "The thing is, some people say they've seen a cloaked figure with glowing, white skin. It's our only clue, but it just sounds crazy. I'm sure it's just a silly rumor made up by people with overactive imaginations. Even still, a few people are wondering if there's a . . . vampire in town."

"Rampire?" Scooby said, shaking inside his armor. "Rikes."

Uncle Brad laughed. "See? It sounds so strange. But I don't have anything else to go on. I just don't know how to solve this mystery."

"Uncle Brad, you know mysteries are our specialty," Daphne said.

"Yeah," Fred chimed in. "We'd be happy to help out."

Uncle Brad scratched his head. "Actually, that's not a bad idea. I could use some fresh ideas. Maybe this case would be a good way for me to show you how things work here at the police station."

The police chief looked outside. The sun had already sunk beneath the rocky cliffs. The orange glow of sunset stretched across the sky. "We can get started in the morning. Why don't you get settled in at the Castle Hotel for the night? I'll see you back here first thing tomorrow."

CHAPTER 2

"Like, this old castle better have room service," Shaggy groaned.

Fred had just parked the Mystery Machine in the lot outside the Castle Hotel. The old hotel was perched on a craggy cliff overlooking the town.

There were no other cars in the lot, and the big, stone building looked dark and spooky. Luckily, the moon was full and shone down on them like a giant flashlight.

"It looks like we're the only guests," Fred said as they walked up to the hotel's big front door.

"Uncle Brad said they don't get a lot of visitors in Castle Rock. This is the only hotel in town." Daphne touched the cracked stone of the castle walls. "Anyway, I think it looks groovy."

"Like, don't they believe in lights at this hotel?" Shaggy wondered aloud.

Velma reached out to open the huge wooden door. But before she touched the handle, the door swung open on its own. "Well, that's interesting," she observed, stepping in.

"More like creepy," Shaggy muttered. "After you, Scoob."

Scooby put his nose to the ground and sniffed his way into the castle. The others followed. When they had all stepped inside, the door creaked closed behind them.

Scooby continued to sniff. A moment later, he bumped into a small, pale man hunched over behind the door. The others didn't notice him until Scooby let out a frightened whimper.

The hunched man stood still and unmoving. He looked tiny next to the huge suits of armor

that stood along the edge of the round stone room. His body was wrapped in a long, cape-like cloak. He stared at the gang silently.

"Hello," Fred said in a friendly voice.

The small, hunched man remained in his place behind the door. He looked at them without a trace of a smile.

"Like, is that guy alive?" Shaggy asked, backing away from the door. He bumped into a suit of armor that toppled over with a clang.

"Yes, yes!" a big, booming voice called from the top of a curving staircase. "He's quite alive. Ivan is our hotel butler. Please, don't mind him. He's very shy. Welcome, welcome! I'm Dr. Franklin, the owner of the Castle Hotel. I'd like to invite you into our majestic home!"

Dr. Franklin swept down the stairs. He was very thin and extremely tall. He had a long, pointed nose and huge ears that stuck out like an elf's. He was wearing a long black cloak that made his skin look ghostly white in the dim entranceway.

"Hello, Dr. Franklin," Fred said. "We would like to stay here tonight. Police Chief Bestler told us you would probably have rooms available?"

"Police Chief Bestler sent you?" The hotel owner looked at them strangely. "Yes, yes, of course. I'm delighted to have you!" When Dr. Franklin smiled, his mouth stretched all the way from one side of his thin face to the other. But suddenly, his smile faded and Dr. Franklin began to sneeze. In less than a minute, he sneezed at least twenty times.

"Are you okay?" Velma asked.

Dr. Franklin continued to sneeze. He held up his hand and said, "Yes, yes, I'm fine. It's just that I'm allergic to animals. *All* animals, I'm afraid." He glanced at Scooby, who tried to hide behind a suit of armor.

"Rorry," Scooby said. He hung his head, embarrassed.

"It's no worry. No worry at all," Dr. Franklin said, waving a hand in the air. "It's only a bit of a sneeze. And it's worth it to have guests who want to join Ivan and myself at our fine hotel!"

Dr. Franklin looked around the hotel lobby sadly. The castlelike mansion looked like it had once been grand. But now it was worn down. The suits of armor all had a fine layer of dust. Giant paintings were faded and cracking. A chandelier that hung from the ceiling was missing crystals.

"People used to come from all over the world to stay at our beautiful Castle Hotel. But business has been very slow lately. We just can't compete with water parks and miniature golf." The hotel owner shook his head. "Things have been especially difficult since some of our guests told the newspaper they saw and heard strange things while they were staying here." He chuckled.

"Like, that's not funny," Shaggy whispered to Scooby. "What kind of strange things?"

Dr. Franklin sighed. "It's just an old mansion, full of creaks and squeaks and bumps in the night. Nothing to worry about." He looked at Ivan, and they both smiled. Or Ivan tried to smile, but his mouth couldn't seem to turn in the right direction.

Scooby and Shaggy exchanged a worried look. Fred, Daphne, and Velma laughed nervously.

"If Ivan and I don't find a way to make some money soon," Dr. Franklin continued, "we're going to have to close up the hotel for good. We will just have to leave it to the bats."

"Rats?" Scooby squeaked.

Dr. Franklin began to sneeze again. When he'd finally stopped, he said, "Ivan will show you to your rooms. He will also be happy to get you anything else you need. Won't you, Ivan?"

Ivan didn't say anything. He just shuffled out from behind the door.

As the gang followed the butler through the grand lobby and up the curving stairs, Scooby and Shaggy lagged behind.

"That Ivan guy doesn't seem like he'd be happy to do anything. He's not very friendly," Shaggy said.

Ivan was rushing up the stairs. It almost seemed like he was trying to get away from the gang. They practically had to run to keep up with him.

The butler led them down long hallways and through dark rooms. He was taking them deeper and deeper inside the old hotel. As they walked farther from the front door, the hallways grew dimmer. Shadows stretched out behind them.

The air seemed to get colder with every step.

"Like, I hope this place has a map," Shaggy muttered, looking over his shoulder.

Suddenly, Ivan stopped. A woman was standing in the middle of the hall in front of him. She had her arms stretched out to the sides, making it impossible for them to pass. Like Dr. Franklin and Ivan, she was wearing a heavy cloak.

"It must always be cold in here," Shaggy whispered to Scooby. "Everyone's wearing cloaks. All we have is armor, Scoob. Like, I guess we didn't pack right for this castle after all."

The woman was very beautiful, but her voice was cold and angry. "I see we have guests, Ivan?" she asked, fixing the gang with a hard stare.

"Yes, we're staying at the hotel for a few nights," Fred answered.

"We're visiting Police Chief Bestler," Daphne explained.

"Police Chief Bestler?" the woman snapped. "What business do you have with him?"

"He's Daphne's uncle," Fred explained. "We're going to be helping him out at the police station for a few days."

The woman's eyes grew wide, but then she smiled. "Well, isn't that just grand?"

"Are you also a guest at the hotel?" Velma wondered.

The tall woman laughed. "Ha! A guest! Why, this is my *home*."

Ivan snorted. It was the first time he'd made a sound, and it almost seemed like he was laughing at the woman.

"*I* am Madame Magnificent," the woman declared proudly. "I'm sure you've heard of me. I was once a famous movie star."

"Nope. I've never heard of you," Shaggy said. Velma gave him a stern look.

"You live here, in the Castle Hotel?" Fred asked.

"Why, yes," Madame Magnificent said. "But you shall soon see that this is not a regular hotel. I have lived here for the past ten years. Someday soon, I will have the means to buy this glorious mansion. I will make it grand again!"

With one final laugh, Madame Magnificent disappeared as quickly as she'd appeared.

"Like, where did she go?" Shaggy asked. "She

didn't even tell us where the hotel restaurant is. Or, like, how to order room service! A nice, warm pie sounds good right about now."

But there was no time to chase after the mysterious woman. Ivan had begun to move again. He led the gang through more dark and narrow passageways. Shaggy and Scooby had to hustle to keep up.

After many twists and turns down the hotel's dark hallways, Ivan brought them to their rooms. He left without saying a word.

"This is the strangest hotel I've ever been in," Velma observed. "Don't you think it's a little strange that we're the only people here?"

Scooby nodded. "Rexrept Radame Ragrifirent."

"Madame Magnificent and *Ivan*," Shaggy reminded them. "I've gotta say, this hotel and these people really give me the creeps." He yawned. "Like, I'm ordering room service and calling it a night."

CHAPTER
3

"This old phone doesn't work," Shaggy said after he and Scooby-Doo had settled into their room. Shaggy put the phone to his ear again. "Definitely broken. Looks like we're going to have to find that Ivan guy and ask him for help finding some food in this place."

Scooby gulped. "Rot Rivan."

"We don't have much choice, Scoob. Dr. Franklin said Ivan would be happy to help us if we needed anything. What we *need* is food. Ivan is the only thing standing between you and me and a feast."

"Rokay," Scooby agreed. He put his knight's helmet back on. "Rust rin rase!"

"Like, that's a good idea," Shaggy said. "I'll wear my armor, too. We can pretend we live in the castle, like Madame Magnificent. I just wish we had capes. This really does seem like more of a 'cape castle.'" He shivered. "*Brrr!* It's cold in here."

Shaggy and Scooby crept out into the dark hallway. "Scooby, old pal, am I dreaming? I think I smell pie!" Shaggy exclaimed, poking his nose into the air. "It's coming from over there." He and Scooby hurried down a long hallway, following the smell of apple pie.

After a few minutes, Scooby stopped next to a small door in the wall. He pulled off his helmet and sniffed excitedly. "Rie!"

Shaggy opened the miniature door and poked his head inside. "Look! It's an old dumbwaiter," he said. "This is a special elevator that brings food from the kitchen up to other rooms. There's a little platform inside the wall that can be used as a snack car."

"Rack rar?" Scooby asked, licking his lips. "Ran re ride rit?"

"Like, that's not a bad idea, Scoob!" Shaggy said. "If we can fit in the dumbwaiter, we can just ride it right down to the kitchen. Then we'll be one step closer to that delicious pie!"

Shaggy pulled at the rope inside the wall. It didn't budge. In fact, it almost felt like someone else was pulling the rope from the other side. Scooby grabbed on to Shaggy's arms to help pull.

They grunted and tugged, trying to get the dumbwaiter to move. Instead, the two friends fell back into a heap on the floor.

"Ris rit ruck?" Scooby asked. He brushed at his armor. He was covered in dust from the floor.

"Like, I don't think this thing works, Scoob. We're going to have to find the kitchen the old-fashioned way." Shaggy grinned. "With our noses!"

Shaggy had just closed the door to the dumbwaiter when there was a loud crash inside the wall. Moments later a horrible, screeching whistle rang through the castle.

"Rhat ras rat?" Scooby asked, shaking.

"I don't think I want to know," Shaggy said. "But that's what my stomach is gonna sound like if I don't eat soon. Like, let's get out of here!"

They ran through the shadowy halls of the hotel, searching for the kitchen. The first turn led them into a room full of stuffed bats.

"Reepy!" Scooby cried as they backed out. They raced off in the other direction.

Another crashing sound shook the floors as they ran through the hotel. "I think I know why people said they heard strange sounds when they were staying here. All I can say is, this pie better be worth it!" Shaggy cried.

They turned a corner and ran into Dr. Franklin. In the dark hallway, the hotel owner looked much less friendly than he had just an hour before. Shaggy backed away nervously.

"Why are you out of your room?" Dr. Franklin asked. "Is something wrong?"

"Like, we were hungry?" Shaggy said hopefully.

Dr. Franklin shook his head, frowning. Then he began to sneeze. "I must go," he said, backing away. "The kitchen is that way." He pointed.

"Ivan is there. He will be happy to help you!"

The hotel owner backed around a corner, still sneezing.

Shaggy said, "Like, that was weird. He was in an awfully big hurry to get away from us. But at least now we know where the kitchen is." He rubbed his hands together. "Let's get some munchies and get back to our room before we bump into that creepy Dr. Franklin again!"

The hotel kitchen was small and cramped, but it was much brighter than the rest of the hotel. Scooby and Shaggy looked everywhere, but they couldn't find any pie.

"Like, I was sure I smelled pie," Shaggy complained.

Even though there were no fresh desserts on the counter, there was a big refrigerator. Shaggy pulled it open.

"Hey, Scoob, check it out! I think we found this castle's treasure room!" Shaggy said hungrily. He reached inside the fridge to grab everything he could.

That's when they heard another crashing sound in the walls. This time, the crash sounded much closer. It sounded like it was coming from the wall right next to Scooby!

Scooby leapt forward, accidentally knocking a bowl of strawberries out of Shaggy's hand. The lights in the kitchen flickered. As the bowl hit the floor, the lights went out, leaving Scooby and Shaggy in pitch darkness.

"Scoob?" Shaggy whispered.

"Reah?" Scooby answered.

"Did you turn out the lights?" Shaggy could hear Scooby licking at the strawberries on the floor. He was chomping and munching noisily in the dark.

"Ruh-ruh."

The kitchen was pitch-black and totally silent. Then, suddenly, a loud knocking sound came from the wall.

A candle flickered next to Shaggy's head. The two friends turned toward it.

A shadowy figure wrapped in a thick fur cloak stood in the darkness just steps from Shaggy and Scooby. Most of the creature's head was covered

with a hood, but traces of glowing white skin peeked out around the edges.

The figure said nothing, but moved closer to Scooby and Shaggy. It hissed, and its fur cape brushed against Shaggy's arm. A row of bright, sharp teeth glinted under the cloak.

With one last glance at the creepy, glowing figure, Shaggy dropped all the food in his hands. "Like, run!" he cried. "Scoob, I think we found Castle Rock's vampire!"

CHAPTER 4

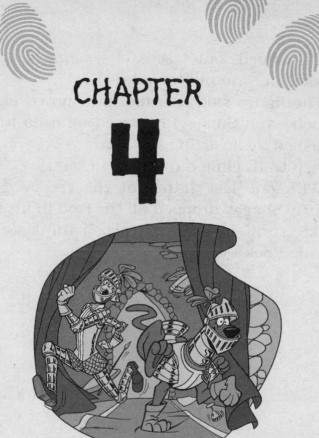

Scooby and Shaggy raced through the hotel's cold, black hallways. They crashed into walls and knocked things onto the floor. Every few steps they bumped into each other, making their armor crash and clang. But the only thing they cared about was getting away from the creepy monster in the kitchen.

After they'd run for a few minutes, Shaggy

stopped short. "I think we can stop running now."

Scooby ran into him, and they fell over into a pile of metal on the floor. They were both out of breath and sweating beneath their armor.

"Zoinks," Shaggy said. "Like, I love dinner guests, but I think that one was more interested in us than he was in real food!"

"Ris rit rone?" Scooby asked, panting.

"I think so," Shaggy said. As he spoke, a candle flickered at the end of the hall. It seemed to be bobbing toward them. Scooby jumped into Shaggy's arms, whimpering.

"Don't worry, Scoob," Shaggy said. "It's just Dr. Franklin."

The hotel owner was holding a bunch of candles in his hands. "Are you all right?" he asked. "I don't know what happened. The electricity seems to have gone out. But there isn't a storm, so I can't understand it."

Dr. Franklin handed Scooby and Shaggy a candle and pointed them in the direction of their room. Without another word, he whipped his cloak around and disappeared down the hall again.

"Like, that guy just keeps getting friendlier and friendlier," Shaggy said. "Let's get back and tell the rest of the gang about that creep in the kitchen."

With the candle as their only light, Shaggy and Scooby had to move slowly through the halls. But a few minutes later, they found their way back upstairs. Fred, Daphne, and Velma were all out in the hall already, searching for candles in the pitch black.

Scooby and Shaggy told them about their adventure. "Like, whatever it was, it was glowing," Shaggy said.

"Reah," Scooby nodded. "Rowing!"

"It was wearing a thick fur cloak!" Shaggy continued, waving his arms in the air. "And it had fangs!"

"Reah! Rike ris!" Scooby flashed his teeth at the gang. He hissed and growled the way the figure in the kitchen had.

"*Hmm,*" Velma said. "A cloak? White skin? That sounds an awful lot like Dr. Franklin. Are you sure it wasn't just Dr. Franklin looking for you because the lights went out?"

Shaggy thought for a moment. He scratched at his head. "Like, I don't know."

"It could have been Ivan." Fred asked. "He wears a cloak, too."

"Raybe," Scooby said.

"Dr. Franklin said that Ivan was in the kitchen, but we didn't see him in there," Shaggy said.

"Madame Magnificent was also wearing a cloak," Daphne pointed out. "It could have been anyone at the hotel." She smiled at Shaggy and Scooby. "I think maybe it just seemed like something scary, since the lights were out."

Shaggy and Scooby looked at each other. Shaggy shivered, thinking about the fur from the cloak brushing against his arm. "Then why didn't that cloaked creature say anything? It just hissed at us!"

"Ivan never speaks," Velma reasoned. "That would explain the hissing."

Shaggy shrugged. "Like, this place still gives me the creeps," he said. "And if my stomach doesn't get some food pronto, it's going to be making some pretty spooky sounds, too!"

Suddenly, Scooby started sniffing again. "Rie!"

"Again?" Shaggy whined, rubbing his stomach. "Scooby and I have been smelling pie all night. It's like someone is trying to torture us!"

"Actually," Daphne said, "I've got good news for you two." She opened the door to her hotel room. When she came back out again, she was holding a hot apple pie. "Ivan delivered this while you were out hunting for the kitchen. He must have heard you say you were hungry."

"Like, why didn't you say something sooner?" Shaggy asked. He handed Daphne the candle so he could grab the pie. "Flaky crust and sweet apples would have made me feel a whole lot better about that creepy old vampire!"

At that moment, a candle flashed at the end of the hall. A cloaked figure stood in the shadows, staring at the gang. The figure's face was hidden under a hood, but glowing white skin and a flash of teeth shone in the candlelight. "Get out," the figure hissed.

Shaggy shook with fear, nearly dropping the pie. "Like, you don't have to tell me twice!"

The figure hissed again before growling, "And stop poking around where you're not welcome!"

Then it blew out the candle and disappeared into the darkness again.

CHAPTER 5

"**P**ie or no pie, I'd say it's time to get out of here. You heard what that thing said," Shaggy moaned. "I'm not spending the night in a vampire hotel!"

"Reah," Scooby said, nodding. "Ret's ro."

"Now wait just a minute," said Fred, holding his hand up. "Remember what Daphne's uncle said about his case? The missing jewels?"

Velma nodded. "Exactly what I was thinking, Fred. The only clue the police have in that case is a cloaked figure with a glowing white face."

"Do you think this vampire and the caped thief are somehow connected?" Daphne asked.

"I don't know," Fred said. "But we promised Police Chief Bestler that Mystery Inc. would help out."

"He meant in the *daylight*," Shaggy moaned. "Like, I'm sure he didn't want us hunting around in a creepy old hotel in the dark."

"Reah," Scooby added.

"Besides, you heard the vampire," Shaggy said, gulping down a big bite of apple pie. "It told us to stop poking around where we're not welcome. I'd say that thing made it pretty clear that we're not welcome."

"There are no other hotels that we can stay at tonight," Fred said. "We might as well look around and see if we can find out a little more about this vampire."

Fred, Daphne, and Velma headed down the hall. Daphne was holding the gang's only candle. So when their friends walked away, Shaggy and Scooby were left in darkness again.

"Safety in numbers?" Shaggy asked Scooby. "Should we go with them?"

"Ruh-huh," Scooby said.

"I'm with you, Scoob," Shaggy agreed. "I don't want to be here in the dark all alone! But first, let's ditch this armor. Like, all it does is get in the way."

Scooby agreed. They quickly removed their armor and ran to catch up with the others.

In the candlelight, everything looked strange and unfamiliar. Within minutes, the gang was lost, and the candle had melted down to a stub. They needed to find Dr. Franklin or Ivan, and fast, or they'd be left in the dark again.

"Where *is* Dr. Franklin?" Daphne wondered.

"And Ivan," Fred added. "He dropped off the pie a few minutes before the lights went off. He must be nearby somewhere."

"He's probably hiding inside a fur cloak, pretending to be a vampire," Shaggy said. "Something about that guy seems super-spooky."

"Maybe we should look inside some of these old rooms," Velma suggested. "I'm sure there must be extra candles somewhere. And maybe we can find the vampire's hiding spot."

"Like, what if the vampire has friends?" Shaggy gulped.

Fred ignored him and opened
an old wooden door at the end
of the hall.

The light of the moon shone in
through the dirty windows inside
the room. Fred and Daphne
peeked inside. "Just an old
library," Fred said.

Velma looked inside the next
room they passed. "This must
be another guest room," she
said. "There's a bed and a
dresser, but nothing else."

When Fred opened the next door, Shaggy and
Scooby poked their heads inside.

"Zoinks!" Shaggy cried.

"Rikes!" Scooby barked.

"What is it, guys?" Fred asked.

"There are, like, headless people in there!"
Shaggy said. The room was filled with people. All
of their bodies were dressed in elaborate outfits,
but none of them had heads.

Velma, Fred, and Daphne looked inside. "Those
are just mannequins," Fred explained. "They're
mannequins wearing old costumes."

Daphne carried the candle inside the room.
It was just light enough for the gang to take a
better look at the mannequins. Some of them

were wearing dresses, but most were clothed in spooky costumes. There was a werewolf, a tattered zombie, and a witch's robe and hat.

"That's interesting," Velma said suddenly, pointing to a dark corner. "One of the costumes is missing!"

"I wonder if this is where our vampire found its cloak?" Fred wondered.

"Maybe you should just ask the vampire!" Shaggy cried. "Like, look!"

Everyone turned. There, in the doorway, stood the hooded creature. This time, it was almost close enough that they could see a face beneath the furry hood.

Fred reached out to try to pull the cape off the creature. But before he could grab hold, the cloaked figure stepped out of the room.

Suddenly, the candle in Daphne's hand went out. They were left in darkness.

CHAPTER
6

After the candle went out, no one moved. Luckily, the moonlight was bright enough that it wasn't completely black. But the mannequins cast creepy shadows all around the room.

Suddenly, a grumbling sound echoed from the corner. Everyone jumped.

"Just my tummy," Shaggy said.

"You just ate an apple pie," Daphne reminded him.

"Like, that just means the *dessert* part of my stomach is full. But the *sandwich* part of my belly is still starving," Shaggy explained.

"There's something strange about that vampire," Fred said. He moved toward the door. "I think it's time for us to split up and look for clues."

"Before we can do that, we need to find another candle," Daphne reminded him.

"We won't be able to follow the vampire's trail in the dark," Velma agreed.

Suddenly, Dr. Franklin appeared. "There you are!" he cried, giving everyone a fresh candle. It was almost as though he had been listening outside the door. He didn't look very surprised to see them. "What on earth are you doing in here? These costumes are awfully scary, aren't they?" He grinned.

"We noticed that one of the costumes is missing," Velma said.

"Yes, yes," Dr. Franklin said. He looked at the empty mannequin. "You're right about that."

"Do you happen to know if it was a vampire costume?" Fred asked.

"A vampire costume?" Dr. Franklin asked. "Why on earth would you ask that?" Suddenly, the hotel owner started sneezing again. He backed toward the door. "I'm sorry," he said nervously. "I must excuse myself."

"Wait, Dr. Franklin!" Fred called after him. "Who do these costumes belong to? Why are they here?"

But Dr. Franklin had already hustled off down the hall.

"He sure was acting suspicious," Velma said.

"Do you think Dr. Franklin is trying to scare us away?" Daphne asked.

"It's possible," Fred said. "But the question is, why? Daph, let's try to track down Ivan, Dr. Franklin, and Madame Magnificent to ask them some questions. Velma, you take Scooby and Shaggy and see if you can follow the vampire's tracks. We need to figure out what this vampire is hiding!"

"Ro ray," Scooby said, shaking his head.

"Like, Scooby and I have been running from that creepy vampire all night," Shaggy said. "There's no way I'm going to go looking for it again. Fool me once, shame on you. Fool me twice, shame on me. Fool me three times, well . . . I don't want to think about seeing that vampire a third time. That would make me a real fool."

"The first time you saw the vampire was in the kitchen," Velma reminded him. "That's probably where we need to start our search."

"Rhe ritchen?" Scooby asked.

Shaggy thought about the bowl of strawberries he'd had in his arms when they'd first seen the cloaked figure. It was probably still all in the kitchen, just waiting for him.

"I guess it couldn't hurt to look for clues in the kitchen," he agreed. "It's not like the vampire is going to be back in there, looking for a cheese sandwich."

"Okay," Fred nodded. "While we search for the others, we'll also try to get the lights back on. It seems mighty suspicious that the electricity went out for no reason at all. It's time to get to the bottom of this!"

Fred and Daphne headed off to find the castle's residents. Shaggy and Scooby led Velma toward the kitchen. The strawberries were still in a pile on the floor, right where Shaggy had dropped them.

"I guess this vampire isn't big on cleaning up," Shaggy said. "Hey, Scoob, do you think this floor is clean?" He looked at the strawberries hungrily.

"Ruck," Scooby said.

"Hey, old pal, you were eating strawberries when the lights went out last time we were here," Shaggy said. "Like, I could hear you licking them off the floor."

"Rot re!" Scooby insisted.

"You heard someone eating when the lights went out?" Velma asked.

"I'd know the sound of someone enjoying a tasty snack anywhere," Shaggy said. "Someone was eating. Like, I was sure it was Scooby-Doo, cleaning up the strawberries I had dropped on the floor."

"Rit rasn't re," Scooby said.

"So unless there was someone else in here with you, that means you must have heard the vampire eating," Velma said. "But real vampires drink blood, right?" She opened the fridge and poked her candle inside. "I don't see any bottles of blood in here, which means our mysterious vampire was eating something else."

"Randriches?" Scooby asked.

"I don't know," Velma said. "But if that cloaked

creep was eating regular food, then it means our vampire really must be a person wearing a disguise. And whoever is under the disguise is trying to scare us away."

Shaggy felt something furry against his arm. "Hey, Scoob, that tickles," he said, laughing.

"Rhat rickles?" Scooby asked. His voice came from all the way across the kitchen. He was nowhere near Shaggy.

Shaggy looked over and saw the vampire's long, fur-cloaked arm reaching for him. "I told you to get out," the figure hissed. "Stop poking around!"

"Like, you're the one poking me!" Shaggy giggled. Then he shrieked. "I guess that vampire *did* have to tell me to get out twice. Like, this time, I'm listening!"

Shaggy started running. "Scooby! Velma! We've gotta go!"

But Shaggy was going nowhere fast. He slipped on the strawberries that were still on the floor. Scooby was just steps ahead of him when they spun out of the kitchen. The vampire chased them down the hall. Velma had run off in the other direction.

Scooby and Shaggy crashed through the hotel's dark halls. The vampire was close on their heels, reaching and grabbing for them. Their candle had long since gone out, so Shaggy grabbed Scooby's tail and let him lead them through the dark with his nose. The hooded creature chased them all the way to the end of a long hallway.

"It's a dead end!" Shaggy cried. The monster was coming closer to them in the darkness. Just then, Shaggy pushed open the only door at the end of the hall. He and Scooby rushed in and slammed the door behind them. "That was close!"

The two friends were in some sort of living room. There were ornate couches, shelves filled with books, and delicate vases perched on tables. The walls were covered in thick drapes.

Shaggy and Scooby pressed against the door

to try to keep the vampire from following them inside. But then they heard a key turning the lock—*click!*—from the outside.

Shaggy gulped. "Like, Scoob? I think that caped creep locked us in here." He reached for the doorknob and turned. The door didn't budge. "We're the vampire's prisoners!"

"Ruh-roh," Scooby said.

"That's what I was thinking," Shaggy agreed. "Well, at least the vampire is out there. And hey, look! Someone left candles . . . and food!"

There were two room service trays sitting in the middle of the room. The trays were covered with silver domes. Shaggy ran over and pulled the top off the first tray. Underneath, there was a platter full of food.

Shaggy rubbed his tummy. "Do you think Ivan left this for us?"

Scooby poked his nose around the platter. Something didn't smell quite right. He began to sneeze, and his eyes watered. His stomach gurgled uneasily.

"Like, I'm not one to turn down a meal, but what is this?" Shaggy asked. He dipped a spoon into a bowl of thick, red liquid.

"Rorms!" Scooby cried. The strange red soup was full of worms.

"What's this?" Shaggy wondered, poking at

a sandwich. It was slimy, and green stuff was oozing out of it. "It smells like stinky feet! Either this is the vampire's meal, or someone's trying to scare us. And the fastest way to do that is by scaring our stomachs so bad we can't even eat!"

"Raggy?" Scooby said. His voice was quivering.

Shaggy looked nervous. "Like, there's something scary behind me, isn't there?" Scooby shook his head and pointed straight up in the air. "Rook!"

All around the room, bats hung from the ceiling. Some had their wings spread wide, while others were tucked up in a sleeping position. In the candlelight, Shaggy could see hundreds of glowing red eyes staring at them.

"Like, I think we might be trapped in the vampire's lair." Shaggy gulped. "And we might be the next thing on the menu!"

CHAPTER 7

"Mind if I join you?" Velma stepped out from behind a curtain. Shaggy and Scooby stared at her. Then they stared at the door. They'd been sure the vampire had locked it.

"Like, how did you get in here?" Shaggy asked.

"When the vampire chased you out of the kitchen, I hid around a corner. Then, when the coast was clear, I returned to the kitchen to try to figure out where that cloaked creep had come from. Let me show you what I found." Velma ducked back behind the curtain.

Scooby and Shaggy looked at each other. "I hope this isn't another trap," Shaggy said. "My stomach still feels funny from the sight of that worm soup. And after smelling that sandwich, I'm not sure I'll ever eat again."

They stepped behind the curtain. It wasn't covering a window, as it had seemed. Instead, the curtain was hiding a secret door. When they stepped through, Velma's candle lit up the room inside.

"Like, this whole room is filled with treasure!" Shaggy cried.

"Rewels!" Scooby said.

"Yes," Velma said proudly. "I have a feeling we've found the jewels that were stolen from the museum, gallery, and people in Castle Rock."

The secret room glistened with jewels. Rubies, emeralds, and diamonds shone in the candle-light. There was a small fortune hidden inside a secret room in the castle!

"How do you think the jewels got here? Like, who could have taken them?" Shaggy asked.

"That's what I'm not sure of yet," Velma said. "I have a hunch about who might be our thief—and our vampire. But let's look for Daphne and Fred, and see what they found."

Velma led Shaggy and Scooby back out of the secret room through a door on the other side of the room. That door took them into a narrow hallway that led them straight back to the kitchen. It was almost like a secret passageway. "I think this part of the castle was once the maid's quarters," Velma explained. "It's like a series of secret tunnels inside the house."

As they walked back into the kitchen, the lights in the hotel flooded back to life. After the total darkness, the dim castle suddenly felt warm and bright. "Like, it looks like Fred and Daphne must have figured out how to turn the electricity back on," Shaggy said. "Maybe we should celebrate with a quick snack before we head back upstairs."

"I thought you said you'd never eat again," Velma responded. "Besides, we need to find Fred and Daphne. It's time to set a trap for the vampire. We need to unwrap this caped crook for good."

As Velma, Shaggy, and Scooby walked back up the stairs toward their rooms, they heard a dull banging coming from the walls again. Then there was a screeching whistle and a rattling sound.

"Like, this old castle sure makes a lot of creepy noises," Shaggy said. "It almost sounds like there's something knocking *inside* the wall. Scoob and

I heard knocking in the kitchen walls right after the lights went *out*, too." He scratched his head. "It's like this place is haunted by a whole lot more than just a vampire."

Velma, Shaggy, and Scooby rounded the corner. Daphne and Fred were standing in the hall, right next to the small dumbwaiter door. The knocking was even louder now.

"Hey, guys," Fred cried. "Look who we just found!"

Fred pulled the door of the dumbwaiter open, and Ivan climbed out! He was even more hunched over than he had been earlier in the night. He gazed at the gang, but didn't say anything.

"Ivan! Like, what on earth were you doing inside the dumbwaiter?" Shaggy asked.

The hotel butler stared at the gang silently. He pointed at the candle that was still in Fred's hand, then at the lights that glowed dimly overhead. Then he groaned and set off down the hall.

"Well, that was strange," Velma said. She poked her head into the dumbwaiter.

"Sure was," Daphne agreed. "I wonder how long he was stuck in there?"

Velma pushed a switch on the inside of the dumbwaiter. It whirred and spun to life. "Very interesting," she said. "This is an electric dumbwaiter."

"Did you guys find any interesting clues?" Fred asked.

"Well, Scoob and I found the vampire again," Shaggy said, holding his stomach. "And we found out what they eat, too."

"Rand rats," Scooby said. "Rots rof rats."

"Bats?" Daphne asked.

"Bats with glowing, ruby-red eyes!" Shaggy cried.

Scooby opened his eyes wide and flapped his wings like a bat.

"Ruby-red eyes?" Fred asked. "That's strange."

"Rand rary!" Scooby said, shaking.

"There's something even more interesting," Velma said. "I think we've found the stolen jewels that Police Chief Bestler is looking for! The treasure is hidden here in the hotel."

"I bet the cloaked figure that people have seen in town is the same vampire that's creeping around here at the hotel," Fred said.

"If we can trap the person who's trying to scare us away from the Castle Hotel," Daphne declared, "we'll also have our thief."

"That's right, Daph," Fred said. "So what are we waiting for? It's time to find out who's hiding under that furry cloak."

"Good luck with that," Shaggy said, peeking inside the dumbwaiter. "Like, Scooby and I will be in our room if you need us."

"Actually," Velma said, "I've got an idea for how we can catch the cloaked creature. But we're going to need you and Scooby to make it work."

"Ro ray," Scooby said, covering his eyes with his paws.

"Would you do it for a Scooby Snack?" Daphne asked.

Scooby shook his head.

"How about *two* Scooby Snacks?" offered Velma.

Scooby held firm. He shook his head again.
"All right, make it three," said Daphne, smiling.
Scooby looked at Shaggy. His stomach grumbled
and rumbled. "Rokay!"

CHAPTER

8

"All right, gang," Fred said. "First, we need to figure out how we're going to get our vampire to come back out of hiding again."

"I've got an idea that I think might work," Velma said. "The vampire thinks Scooby and Shaggy are still trapped in the sitting room. If I hadn't found the secret way into the room to let them out, they'd still be stuck in there."

"Thanks for rescuing us, Velma," Shaggy said. "That room was a total downer."

"I hate to say it, but for this plan to work, we're going to have to sneak you back in," Velma said.

"You want us to go back in the vampire's lair?" Shaggy asked. "Like, why?"

"I think I see where Velma's going with this," Fred interrupted. "If the vampire thinks you're still in the room, whoever is hiding under that creepy cape will have to come back to let you out. They know we're going to come looking for you if you're missing for too long. And our thief is probably worried we'll find the other things they've hidden inside that room when we do."

"But the vampire seems to prefer the dark," Daphne continued, "so to get it to come back out of hiding, we're going to have to turn the lights off again."

"That's a good point, Daphne," Fred said, nodding. "When the castle is dark, the vampire will come back to get Scooby and Shaggy. Then we can catch it. But we need to hurry, or the vampire might come up with a different plan of its own."

"So, let me get this straight," Shaggy asked nervously. "Scooby and I have to just sit there, waiting for the vampire to come back and get us?"

"Don't worry, Shaggy," Velma reassured him. "We'll trap the vampire before it has a chance to do anything to you. You're just the bait."

"Rampire rait?" Scooby asked, swallowing loudly.

"Let's go," Fred said quickly. "Daph, you get the lights. Velma and I will set the trap. Scooby and Shaggy, just try to look delicious." He laughed.

"Delicious? Vampire bait?" Shaggy whined. "Like, that's not very funny."

The others laughed.

"Let's go, gang," Fred called, heading down the hall. "There's no time to lose."

Daphne split off from the others. She was going to turn the electricity in the hotel back off. The rest of the gang headed back through the kitchen toward the vampire's lair. They entered the living room through the secret door. The main door was still locked from the outside.

"We'll wait in here," Fred told Shaggy and Scooby. He and Velma were behind the curtains, inside the room full of jewels. "When the vampire opens the door to let you out, you two need to find some way to lure it inside. Then Velma and I will jump out and trap it."

Moments later, the lights went out again.

"Daphne must have flipped the electrical switch," Velma whispered. "The vampire should be back here any minute."

Shaggy and Scooby sat on the couch, waiting nervously. They watched the door, listening for the click that would tell them the vampire was unlocking it. They sat and stared, but minutes passed and still the vampire didn't return.

"Like, what happens if the vampire doesn't ever come back?" Shaggy asked.

As he spoke, Shaggy felt a fur-covered arm around his neck. The vampire was standing directly behind them!

Scooby jumped off the couch just in time to escape the vampire's clutches. But Shaggy was trapped, held in place by the vampire's long arms.

The vampire started tying Shaggy up. He squirmed and wriggled, but the vampire held him tight.

"Don't worry," the vampire hissed. "I found your little friends, too, and they're all tied up. No one is going to rescue you this time."

But the vampire had forgotten about Scooby! All of a sudden, he leaped up on one of the room-service trays. The force of his jump made the tray roll forward—toward Shaggy and the vampire!

With a loud *splat*, the rolling tray hit the vampire squarely in the stomach. Wormy red soup flew into the air. It covered the vampire's white skin, dripping everywhere like blood. The oozing, stinky sandwich landed with a *plop* on the top of the vampire's hood.

The cloaked creature let out a high-pitched scream. "My makeup! My costume!"

While the vampire hollered and wiped at its face, Shaggy jumped up and shook off the rope that was wrapped around his hands. The vampire hadn't had time to knot it yet.

"Shaggy! Scooby! In here!" Fred cried from behind the curtain.

Scooby stood watch over the vampire while Shaggy poked his head inside the secret door. Fred, Daphne, and Velma were all tied up together, sitting on a pile of jewels. Both of the girls had gags in their mouths. Fred had just managed to shake his free.

"Like, this wasn't exactly the plan," Shaggy said as he untied his friends.

"I ran into the vampire while I was turning off the electricity," Daphne explained. "I was caught by surprise, which gave our caped creature an advantage. The vampire gagged me and dragged me here."

Fred continued the story. "Velma and I were caught by surprise, too. Instead of going back to its lair through the main door, like we'd expected, the vampire sneaked in through the secret passage. Velma and I were tied up and trapped in here before we could warn you."

"I guess we're going to have to come up with another trap to catch the vampire," Velma said sadly.

"I can't believe our plan didn't work," Fred said.

"Like, not so fast!" Shaggy said, pushing aside the curtain between the two rooms. "I'm happy to say that room service—and my old pal Scooby-Doo—saved the day!"

CHAPTER
9

F red, Daphne, Velma, and Shaggy hurried
back into the living room. Scooby-Doo was
sitting on top of the vampire.

"Great work, Scooby." Fred said, bringing a
candle closer. "Okay, gang, let's see who's hiding
under that fur cloak!"

Daphne reached forward and pulled back

the vampire's hood. "Madame Magnificent!" she cried.

"Just as I suspected," Velma said.

Madame Magnificent narrowed her eyes at the gang. "This is not the way to treat a famous actress," she cried, spitting a worm out of her mouth. "I demand a costume change!"

Just then, Ivan and Dr. Franklin hurried into the sitting room. "What's going on in here?" Dr. Franklin said. "What on earth are you doing in a pool of tomato soup, Madame Magnificent?"

"Dr. Franklin, we'll explain everything," Fred said. "But first we need to call Police Chief Bestler. I think we've found something he's been looking for."

● ● ●

Fifteen minutes later, Police Chief Bestler arrived at the old hotel. The gang quickly told him about their night and showed him the room full of stolen jewels. Madame Magnificent sat angrily under her wet cloak. Scooby was still keeping a close eye on her.

"I can't believe you solved our case!" Daphne's uncle said. He patted Daphne's shoulder proudly.

"But how on earth did you know it was Madame Magnificent, Velma?" Shaggy asked. "Like, no offense, but everyone in this hotel seemed a little suspicious to me."

"You're right, Shaggy. At first, it seemed like it could be anyone," Velma agreed. "The vampire was wearing a cloak, but that didn't narrow things down at all."

"It's very cold in the hotel," Dr. Franklin said. "We all wear cloaks to keep warm."

"Right," Velma said. "The first real clue we found was in the mannequin room. It wasn't until later that we realized all of those costumes must be Madame Magnificent's old movie costumes. I bet you played a vampire in one of your movies?" She glanced at Madame Magnificent, who nodded proudly.

"The next clue was the electric dumbwaiter," Velma continued, looking at Ivan the butler.

"Rhe rumbraiter?" Scooby said.

"Like, what does the dumbwaiter have to do with anything other than Ivan and that delicious pie?" asked Shaggy.

Velma held one finger in the air. "Exactly. Ivan is so small that he could ride in the dumbwaiter to bring the pie up to your room. Then, just as he started to ride back down to the kitchen, the power was switched off and the dumbwaiter stopped."

Daphne spoke up. "If the dumbwaiter stopped working when the electricity went out, then that means Ivan must have been stuck inside the wall the whole time the lights were off!" She looked at Ivan. He nodded. "Poor Ivan."

Velma continued. "I put two and two together when Shaggy told me he and Scooby had heard knocking sounds coming from the wall after the electricity went off. I realized the knocking must have been Ivan, calling for help. That's when I knew he couldn't possibly have been the vampire. He was trapped inside the wall the whole time the vampire was chasing us."

Ivan's pale face turned red. He ducked his head, embarrassed that people were talking about him.

"And it was easy to rule out Dr. Franklin," Fred chimed in. "Because of his allergies, he starts sneezing whenever Scooby's nearby. Plus, Shaggy, you told us the vampire's cloak was made out of fur. If it was Dr. Franklin hiding under there, that would have been a very sneezy vampire."

"Very smart," Dr. Franklin said, beaming. "Very smart, indeed. But, Madame Magnificent, why did you do this?"

Madame Magnificent lifted her head. "I had jewels hidden everywhere in the hotel." She glanced up at the bats hanging from the ceiling in the sitting room. Now that the lights were back on, the gang could see that the room was filled with fake bats whose eyes were made out of rubies.

"Wow!" Daphne exclaimed. "You really did have jewels hidden everywhere!"

Madame Magnificent continued. "I had to keep you nosy kids from poking around, so I tried to scare you away from my hiding places. I put my old acting chops to good use. I set a perfect scene, designed the perfect costume, and practiced my sound effects. It all came together perfectly!" She laughed bitterly. "I was going to use the money I made selling the stolen jewels to buy the Castle Hotel. I am a movie star, and I deserve to live like the star that I am. I don't want to live in this old, rundown hotel anymore!"

"You don't have to worry about that," Police Chief Bestler said. He wrapped handcuffs around her wrists. "Your new home is going to be the county jail!"

Madame Magnificent squirmed. "I was *this close* to scaring you away from *my* home and *my* treasure, for good!" She hissed, which made her sound just like the vampire. "I would have gotten away with it, too, if it weren't for you meddling kids and that miserable fur ball."

Police Chief Bestler led Madame Magnificent away.

"I have an idea for you, Dr. Franklin," Daphne said. "This old castle really is groovy. What if you turned it into a haunted hotel?"

"You mean, a theme hotel?" Dr. Franklin asked. "With fake vampires and ghosts and other spooky stuff?"

"That's exactly what I was thinking," Daphne said. "Some people like to be scared. A good gimmick might help you get more visitors."

Dr. Franklin smiled. "Yes, yes! That's not a bad idea! Thanks, Daphne."

"Well, Scoob, I think a long night of police work has earned us a donut or ten," Shaggy said. "What do you say, old pal?"

"Reah, ronuts!" Scooby cried, licking his lips. "Scooby-Dooby-Doo!"